P9-DMO-194

Millions of Americans remember Dick and Jane (and Sally and Spot too!). The little stories with their simple vocabulary words and warmly rendered illustrations were a hallmark of American education in the 1950s and 1960s.

But the first Dick and Jane stories actually appeared much earlier—in the Scott Foresman Elson Basic Reader Pre-Primer, copyright 1930. These books featured short, upbeat, and highly readable stories for children. The pages were filled with colorful characters and large, easy-to-read Century Schoolbook typeface. There were fun adventures around every corner of Dick and Jane's world.

Generations of American children learned to read with Dick and Jane, and many still cherish the memory of reading the simple stories on their own. Today, Pearson Scott Foresman remains committed to helping all children learn to read—and love to read. As part of Pearson Education, the world's largest educational publisher, Pearson Scott Foresman is honored to reissue these classic Dick and Jane stories, with Grosset & Dunlap, a division of Penguin Young Readers Group. Reading has always been at the heart of everything we do, and we sincerely hope that reading is an important part of your life too.

Dick and Jane

We Play and Pretend

The scanning, uploading, and distribution of this book via the Internet or via any other means without the permission of the publisher is illegal and punishable by law. Please purchase only authorized electronic editions, and do not participate in or encourage electronic piracy of copyrighted materials. Your support of the author's rights is appreciated.

Dick and Jane® is a registered trademark of Addison-Wesley Educational Publishers, Inc. From FUN WITH OUR FRIENDS. Copyright © 1962 by Scott, Foresman and Company. All rights reserved.

Published in 2005 by Grosset & Dunlap, a division of Penguin Young Readers Group, 345 Hudson Street, New York, New York 10014. GROSSET & DUNLAP is a trademark of Penguin Group (USA) Inc. Printed in China

ISBN 978-0-448-43615-9   10 9 8 7 6 5 4 3 2

Dick
and
Jane

We Play and Pretend

GROSSET & DUNLAP • NEW YORK

CONTENTS

The Hat

Jane said, "Dick! Dick!
Can you do this?"

Dick said, "Look at the hat!
See what I can do!
Can you do this, Jane?"

"Where is the hat?" said Dick.
"Do you see it?
Where is it?"

Jane said, "I see the hat!
Do you see where it is, Dick?
Come and see where the hat is.
Look at Pete!"

Sally and Billy

Sally said, "This is fun.

This is fun for Billy and me.

We like to play with you, Pete."

Billy said, "We like to play.

We like to play with you, Pete."

Billy said, "Do this!
Do this!"

Sally said, "Look, Pete.
Look at me.
I like to do this.
Can you do it?"

"Yes, I can," said Pete.

Pete said, "Now look at me.
See what I can do."

Sally said, "Help! Help!
Come and help me, Dick."

Billy said, "Help! Help!"

Sally said, "Thank you, Dick."

Billy said, "Thank you, Spot."

Pete said, "I do not thank Spot.
See where Spot is!
This is no help to me!"

Work to Do

Dick said, "Hello, Father.
What is that?
Can I help you with it?"

"Yes, thank you," said Father.
"Get to work, Dick."

Jane said, "What is that, Dick?
Is it for us?
Can we play with it?"

"No, Jane," said Dick.
"We can't play with this.
But you will like it.
We can have fun with it."

Sally said, "Get away, Jane!
Get away!
I can't see what that is.
Spot and I want to look at it."

Father said, "Not now, Sally.
You and Jane go away.
Go and play with Spot.
I have work to do."

Sally said, "Help! Help!
I want to get out!"

Jane said, "Get away, Dick.
I can't see now."

Dick said, "You can't see.
But Father can.
Now Father can see to work."

Mother Helps Pete

Pete said, "Look out!
Look out for the ball!"

"I have it, Pete," said Father.
"Come and get it.
We can't eat this."

"Hello, Pete!" said Dick.
"Come and see what we have.
It is fun to eat out here."

Mother said, "Hello, Pete!
Do you want to eat with us?"

Pete said, "Oh, yes, thank you!
I do want to, and maybe I can.
I will go and see my mother."

Pete said, "Hello!
Here I come.
I can eat with you."

Father said, "Good!
Come and help us.
We have work to do."

"This is not work," said Dick.
"This is fun."

"Here, Pete," said Mother.

"Have one.

Have a big one."

Pete said, "No, thank you!

I want one, but I can't eat it.

Look at this!"

Mother said, "Maybe I can help.
See what I can do.
Can you eat this now?"

Pete said, "Oh, yes!
I can eat that."

"Good!" said Dick.
"You can eat that.
And I can eat this big one."

A Good Dog

"No, Puff, no!" said Dick.

"Go away! Go away, Puff!
Pete and I want the red ball.
You can't help us find it."

Pete said, "I see a little blue ball.
But I can't find a red one in here."

Dick said, "Where is that red ball?
I can't find it."

"Spot can!" said Pete.
"Here comes Spot with the red ball."

"Hello, Spot," said Dick.
"You are a good dog!
Thank you for the red ball."

Pete said, "Look, Dick.

Spot wants something in there.

What can that dog want?"

Dick said, "I will find out.

My little blue ball is in there.

Maybe Spot wants that."

Pete said, "Oh my!
There is Puff."

Dick said, "Good for you, Spot!
Pete and I did not see Puff in there."

Pete said, "You are a good dog, Spot.
You are a good dog!
You are a big help to us."

Two Funny Girls

"Girls! Girls!" said Mother.
"Come in the house now.
I have something for you."

Jane said, "Oh, Mother!
What do you have for us?"

"Come and find out," said Mother.
"I have something pretty for you."

Jane said, "What pretty coats!
I like the blue one.
I look good in blue."

"I like the red coat," said Sally.
"I will look pretty in it."

Sally said, "Look at me!
Do I look pretty in my red coat?"

"No, Sally," said Jane.
"That red coat is too big for you.
Maybe the red coat is for me.
We will see."

Sally said, "This red coat looks funny.
That blue coat looks funny on you, too.
You do not look pretty in it."

Jane said, "Oh, Sally!
The coats are not funny.
We did something funny.
The big red coat is for me.
This little blue one is for you."

The Little House

"Easy now!" said Tom.

"We want this house to look good."

"It will," said Dick.

"You and I can have fun in it."

"Oh, Susan!" said Jane.

"Can we play in that little house?"

Tom said, "Dick and I are in here.
You two girls can't come in now.
This house is too little."

"See what I did!" said Susan.

"I put something on the house."

"What is that?" said Tom.

Susan said, "Can't you guess?
Can't you guess what it is?"

"I can't guess," said Tom.
"I can't guess," said Jane.

"Look up there!" said Dick.

"Look up there, Tom!

Do you see what I see?

Can't you guess what Susan did?"

"Now I can," said Tom.

"Thank you, Susan.

I like that on the little house.

It looks good."

Here We Go

"Come on!" said Pete.

"Here we go.

One, two! One, two!"

Billy said, "This coat is too big.

I don't want to play."

Pete said, "Yes, you do.

One, two! One, two!"

"I can't see," said Sally.

"I don't want this hat on me.
I don't want to play."

"Look out, Pete!" said Susan.
"Look out for Puff and Spot!"

Pete said, "Will do. Will do.
One, two! One, two!"

Pete said, "Oh, oh!
Down we go!"

"Oh, Pete!" said Jane.
"You did not look out for Spot!"

"I can't get up," said Billy.
"Help me up!
Please help me up!"

Pete said, "Here, Spot!
I want that!
You can't have it."

"Yes, you can," said Sally.
"Run, Spot, run!
Run fast!
Now Billy and I don't have to play."

Spot Finds Something

"Spot! Spot!" said Dick.
"Put that hat down!
That is Sally's hat.
Put it down, Spot.
Please put it down!"

"Here, Jane," said Dick.

"Here is Sally's hat.

Will you please take it to the house?

I want to play ball with Tom."

Jane said, "Oh, Dick.

I don't want to put Sally's hat away.

I want to play with Susan."

"Come here, Sally," said Jane.

"Please take this hat to the house."

"I want to ride now," said Sally.

"I will take my hat to Dick.

Maybe Dick will take it to the house."

Sally said, "Here, Dick.

Will you put my hat away?

I want to ride on my horse."

Tom said, "Come on, Dick.

Please come on and play ball.

That is Sally's hat.

Sally can put it away."

"Here, Spot," said Dick.

"You take Sally's hat to the house.

You are the one to do this."

Sally said, "Run to the house, Spot!

Take my hat to Mother.

Run, Spot, run!"

Get a Horse

"See my horse run," said Sally.
"Away I go for a fast ride."

Tom said, "Put that horse down, Sally.
Dick and I will take you for a ride.
You can ride fast on this train."

Sally said, "Here is Pete.
Pete can ride on the train.
I will ride on my horse."

Pete said, "Hello!
That looks like a good train.
Do you want my blue wagon for it?"

"Thanks," said Dick.
"That blue wagon will help."

"Look here, Sally," said Tom.
"See what a good train we have.
Come and ride with us."

Dick said, "Jump in a wagon, Sally.
Jump in the wagon with Spot.
We will take you for a fast ride.
Come and get on the train."

"No, no!" said Sally.

"Puff can ride in the wagon with Spot.

I want to ride on my horse.

Look here, boys.

My horse can go fast.

It can jump, too.

Here we go.

Jump, jump, jump!"

Dick said, "Oh, oh!
We don't have a fast train now.
This train can't take us home."

Sally said, "Get a horse, boys.
Get a horse.
A horse will take you home."

Susan Reads a Book

Pete said, "Hello, Tom.

Hello, Susan.

Come and play with us."

Susan said, "Not now, Pete.

I want to read this book.

Tom will play with you boys."

Tom said, "Come on, Susan.
Please don't read that book now.
You can read at home."

"Not this book," said Susan.
"I can't read it at home.
This is not my book.
I have to read it here."

Susan said, "Help me read this.
The dog in this book runs away.
But it jumps on something and
rides home.
I want to know what it rides on."

"Oh, Susan," said Tom.
"I can't help you now.
I want to play with Pete."

Susan said, "I want to know
what this dog rides on."

"On a train!" said Billy.
"That dog rides home on a train."

Susan said, "Billy! Can you read?"

"No," said Billy.
"I can't read, but my mother can.
She reads that book to me."

Tim Takes a Ride

Dick said, "Look there, Pete.

There is Tim in Sally's car.

Let's do something funny with the car."

Pete said, "We will have to work fast.

We don't want Sally to see us."

Sally said, "Tim! Tim!
I want my car.
Please don't take it away."

Jane said, "Oh, Sally!
Tim can't take the car away.
Let's find out who did take it.
Come with me, Sally."

"Oh, boys!" said Sally.

"Tim did not take my car.

You boys did, and I know

how you did it.

Please take Tim and me home now.

Let's see how you do that!"

How Funny We Look!

Pete said, "My! I look funny."

Tom said, "We all look funny.
Look at Jane and me.
See how big we are."

Pete said, "See what I did.

Look at Jane now.

Guess who she looks like."

"She looks like Mother," said Dick.

"Let's see what you can do to me.

Who can you make me look like?"

Pete said, "Here you are, Dick.
Do you know who you look like?"

"I look like me," said Dick.
"That is a big funny me."

Jane said, "Oh, yes, that is Dick.
He likes to play ball."

Tom said, "Now do me, Pete.
Make me look funny."

Pete said, "How do you like that?"

"Oh, that is good!" said Tom.
"Now make a horse for me."

Pete said, "I can't.
I don't know how to make animals."

Dick said, "Now let's make
Pete look funny.
I know what I can do to Pete."

Jane said, "Come here, Father.
See how funny Pete looks.
See how funny we all look."

"Yes, I see," said Father.
"Who knows what you have to do now?"

"We all know," said Dick.

Sally Helps Mother

Jane said, "One, two, three for Dick.
Now he is **It**."

Dick said, "Here are Mother and Father.
Maybe they will play with us."

Jane said, "This wagon is **Home.**
You have to run here to get Home."

Dick said, "Now you can all go.
I will come and find you."

Away ran Father and Sally.
Away ran Mother and Jane.

Dick went to look for Father.

But Father and Sally ran Home.

"One, two, three for me!" said Father.

"And one, two, three for Sally!"

Dick went to find Jane.

But she ran to the wagon.

"One, two, three for me!" she said.

Away went Dick to find Mother.

Sally said, "Run fast, Mother!
Run Home!
I will help you.
Here I come with the wagon."

Dick said, "Don't do that, Sally!
I know you want to help Mother.
But that is not how we play."

Who Knows?

Susan said, "What a funny blue cat!
Can we play with it?"

Jane said, "Yes, we can play with it.
But I don't want Spot to see it.
Spot likes to play with my animals.
He will take my blue cat and
run away with it."

"I like this little dog," said Susan.
"Can we play with it?"

Jane said, "Oh, yes.
I have a little horse, too.
I will get it out.
Then we can play with all
three animals."

The girls did not see Dick.
They did not see what he did.

"Where is my blue cat?" said Jane.
"I put it down there."

"I know it was there," said Susan.
"Did Spot come in and get it?"

"Maybe he was in here!" said Jane.
"Let's go out and look for Spot."

Then out went Jane and Susan.
Out they ran to find Spot and the cat.

"Look up there!" said Jane.
"There is my blue cat!
How did it get up there?"

"Who knows?" said Susan.
"I don't.
But I know Spot did not put
that cat up there."

Pete's Birthday

"Hello," said Pete.
"Come in, come in."

Tom said, "Here, Pete.
Susan and I have something for you."

"Oh, thank you!" said Pete.
"Come on in."

Sally said, "Happy birthday, Pete.
This is for you."

Then Dick said, "Hello, Pete.
Jane and I have something for you, too.
Happy birthday!"

Pete was a happy boy.

He said, "I like this little car.

I like the three animal books, too.

I read all the animal books I can get.

Thank you! Thank you!"

Pete's mother said, "It is time to eat.

Will you all come in here now?"

"Oh, yes," said the boys and girls.

Then they all went in to eat.

"Happy birthday to you.
Happy birthday to you.
Happy birthday, dear Pete.
Happy birthday to you!"

Look Out!

Jane said, "I want to ride on that.
Do you want to go with me, Dick?"

"Yes," said Dick.
"That looks like fun.
Let's have a ride on it."

Dick said, "I can see all the park.
Look down there, Jane.
Do you see Susan?"

"Yes, I do!" said Jane.
"I see Tom, too.
But they don't see us."

"Hello, Tom," said Dick.
"Hello, down there."

Susan said, "Look out, Tom!
Look out!
Oh dear!"

All Tom said was "Oh!"

Who Can Get a Duck?

Jane said, "I like that duck.
Where did you get it, Tom?"

"Here in the park," said Tom.
"You can get one, but you
will have to work for it."

Father said, "Come on, Jane.
I will get a duck for you."

"I want the white duck," said Jane.
"Try to get that one for me, Father."

"I can try three times," said Father.
"Maybe I can get the white duck.
One! Two! Three!"

"No white duck!" said Jane.
"No duck at all!"

"Dick, you try now," said Father.
"Let's see what you can do."

"One!" said Dick.

"No duck!" said Jane.

"Two!" said Dick.

"No duck!" said Jane.

"Three!" said Dick.

"No duck!" said Jane.
"No duck for me."
She was not happy.

"Now Jane can try," said Dick.
"Maybe she can get the white duck."

Father said, "Maybe she can.
Go on and try, Jane."

"One!" said Jane.
"Oh, I got it! I got it!
I got my white duck."

"Yes, you did," said Father.
"And you got it with one try."

Time to Go Home

Father said, "Where is Jane?
It is time to go home now."

"I know where Jane is," said Dick.
"She went back to see the ducks."

Dick ran to get Jane.
He looked and looked, but he
did not find her.

Father said, "Here comes Jane,
but Dick is not with her.
I will have to go back and find him."

"Let me go," said Sally.
"Dick is here in the park.
I can find him."

"No, Sally," said her mother.
"I don't want you to go away.
Dick will come back here.
He knows we want to go home."

"Dick came back!" said Sally.
"Here he is."

"Yes," said Father.
"Dick came back.
You are all three here now.
Don't run away.
We have to go home."

Dick said, "Here, girls.
Take this and don't let go.
Then we will all go with Father."

Father said, "Good for you, Dick!
Here we all go to the car!"

Something for Billy

"Hello, Pete," said Dick.
"Jane and I came to get a new book.
Do you want a book, too?"

"No," said Pete.
"Billy wants something new
to play with.
I came to help him get it."

Jane said, "Look here, Billy.
Here is a pretty little rabbit.
This is a good toy.
Do you want it?"

Billy looked at the rabbit.
Then he said, "No, thank you.
I don't want a toy rabbit.
I don't like toy animals."

Pete said, "Come here, Billy.

Look at this toy farm.

Do you want me to get it for you?"

Billy came and looked at the toy farm.

Then he said, "No, thank you.

I don't want a toy farm.

I want something that can go.

Help me find a new toy that will go."

Dick looked at the games.

He said, "Come here, Pete.

Here is a good new game.

Maybe Billy will like this."

Pete said, "We have that game at home.

I got it for my birthday.

Billy is too little to play with it.

He wants a toy that will go.

Let's find one for him."

"Oh, Billy!" said Jane.

"You don't want a toy rabbit.

You don't want a toy farm.

You don't want a new game.

You are not easy to please."

"Look here!" said Billy.

"I see what I want."

"That is not a toy," said Pete.

"But look at it go!"

The New Game

"I like this new game," said Susan.

"It is easy to make the clowns go down.
I got all but three."

Pete said, "Let Jane try now.
Then Tom can try.
We have to play one at a time."

Jane had a try, but not one clown
went down.

"Oh dear!" she said.

"This new game is not easy for me."

Then Tom had a try.

"Look!" he said.

"I got all but one clown."

Then Dick had a try.

He got all but two clowns.

"Hello, Billy," called Dick.

"Come and try to play this new game."

Billy said, "Not me!
I can't play that game.
I will play with my wagon."

"Come on, Billy," called Tom.
"This new game is fun.
Try to make the clowns go down.
Then you can play with the wagon."

Billy came and had a try.

"See what I did!" he said.

"Pete, you take my yellow ball.
Then you can make all the clowns
go down."

Pete said, "No, thanks, Billy.
We can't play with the big yellow ball.
We have to play with the little ball.
It came with the game."

Away to the Farm

Jane said, "Hello, hello!
Come in, Grandfather, come in.
Did you come to get Dick?"

"Yes, Jane," said Grandfather.
"I came to get him and Pete.
I want to take the boys home with me."

"My, my!" said Grandfather.
"That yellow cake looks good."

Mother said, "It is for Dick's birthday.
I want you to take it home with you."

"Good!" said Grandfather.
"Do you girls want to go to the farm?
You can help eat Dick's yellow cake."

"Yes, yes!" said Jane and Sally.

"Hello, Grandfather," said Dick.

"This is my friend Pete.

I had to go get him."

Grandfather said, "Hello, Pete.

Happy birthday, Dick!

Let's all get in the car now.

It is time to go."

"Here comes Spot," said Dick.

"He wants to go with us."

Grandfather said, "Jump in the car, Spot.
I guess we can take you, too."

"Have a good time!" called Mother.
"Have a good time at the farm."

"Hello, Grandmother!" called Dick.
"Here is my friend Pete."

Then out came Spot and Jane and
Sally and Tim.

"My, my!" said Grandmother.
"Grandfather went to get two boys.
Here are two boys and two girls and
Spot and Tim.
How good it is to have you all here
for Dick's birthday!"

A Funny Cake

Dick said, "Don't go in, Grandfather.
Come with Pete and me.
Pete wants to see the farm."

Grandmother said, "Not now, Dick.
Let's eat now.
Then your friend can see the farm."

Dick said, "Oh my!
I have had all I can eat."

"No, Dick," said Grandfather.
"You have a birthday cake to eat.
Your mother wanted you to eat it here.
We put it in the car at your house."

Then Grandfather went out to the car
to get the big yellow cake.

Grandfather came back to the house, but he did not have the cake.

"Dear me!" he said.

"I did not find your cake, Dick.
I guess it is back at your house.
We can't go back after it now.
What will we do?"

Grandmother got up.
"I know what to do," she said.
"Come and help me, Jane.
We have work to do."

Soon Grandmother and Jane came back.

"Happy birthday!" they said.

"Happy birthday, Dick!"

"What a funny cake!" said Dick.

"But what a good one!"

A Ride on Clown

Jane saw the boys on the black pony.

"Let me ride, too," she called.

Grandfather said, "Not now, Jane.

Three can't get on Clown.

Let the boys ride now.

You can ride after they come back."

Away went the two boys on Clown.

Dick said, "I like Clown.
This is a good, fast ride."

"Look there, Dick!" said Pete.
"There went two rabbits!
Let's jump down and try to find them."

The boys got down to find the rabbits.
Soon they saw the rabbits jump out.
Clown saw them, too!

The black pony ran away,

and the boys ran after him.

"Come back, Clown!" called Dick.

"Come back here!"

But the black pony ran on and on.

"Oh dear!" said Pete.

"What do we do now?"

"We walk!" said Dick.

"Come on, my friend.

We have to walk, walk, walk!"

"Look here, boys," called Jane.
"Clown came back to get me.
He wanted me to have a ride.
He is my friend."

Dick said, "Maybe Clown is
your friend.
But he is not my friend, and he
is not Pete's friend.
He ran away, and Pete and I
had to walk home."

Where Is Sally?

"Sally! Sally!" called Grandmother.
"Come here, Sally."

Jane said, "Sally went for a walk
with Tim.
I guess she went to see the chickens.
She wanted to see them eat."

Dick ran to the chicken house
to get Sally.
He saw big hens in there, but he
did not see Sally.

"Grandmother!" he called.
"Sally is not here.
She is not in the chicken house."

"Oh dear!" said Grandfather.
"Where did Sally go?
We will have to find her."

"Look!" said Grandmother.
"Here comes Boots with Tim.
Boots knows where Sally is."

Grandfather said, "Here, Boots.
Let me have Tim.
Then take us to Sally.
Go on, Boots.
Go find her for us."

Boots looked up at Grandfather
and barked.

Then away he ran.

"Come on, boys," called Grandfather.
"Boots will take us to Sally."

Soon Boots saw Sally.
He barked and barked.
"Boots sees Sally," said Grandfather.
"There she is!"

"Sally, Sally," said Grandfather.
"How did you get out here?"

Sally said, "I went for a walk.
I went to the chicken house.
I saw all the big hens.
Then I saw a pretty little rabbit.
I ran after it, but it got away.
Then I had to look for Tim.
Where did you find him?"

Grandfather said, "We did not find Tim.
It was Boots who did that.
Boots had to help us find you, too."

Fire! Fire!

Grandmother said, "Come down, Sally!
You can't play up there."

Sally said, "Look, Grandmother!
Look at that fire!"

"Oh my!" said Grandmother.
"I will have to put it out!"

Soon Grandmother called, "Sally!
This fire is so big I can't put it out.
Go get your grandfather.
Run, Sally, run!"

Back to the house ran Sally.
"Fire! Fire! Fire!" she called.
"Come fast, Grandfather.
Don't walk! Run!"

Grandfather ran to help Grandmother.
All the children ran after him.

Grandfather said, "Girls! Girls!
Go back where the boys are.
Maybe you can help them."

Dick called, "Come here, Jane.
Come and make the chickens get away.
Then you can work with Pete and me."

The fire was soon out.

"Thank you, boys," said Grandfather.

"Thank you, Jane.
We got that fire out fast."

Sally said, "Thank me, Grandfather.
I did something to help put out the fire."

Jane laughed and said, "Oh, Sally!
How did you help put out the fire?"

"I went to get Grandfather," said Sally.

What a Day!

"Look, Dick," said Pete.
"Your father and mother are here.
They have come after us."

"Hello, there," called Father.
"Did you children have a good day?"

Mother said, "Did you have fun?
What did you do all day?"

"What a day we had!" laughed Pete.
"We looked at all the farm animals.
We saw cows and pigs and chickens.
Then Dick and I had a ride on Clown.
Clown saw two rabbits and ran away.
So Dick and I had to walk home.
We had to walk and walk and walk."

Dick said, "That is not all.
Sally went to see the hens.
Then she saw a rabbit.
She wanted to pet it, so she ran after it.
Boots had to help us find her."

"After that we had a fire," said Jane.
"We all had to help put it out."

Father laughed and said, "My, my!
How did you do all that in one day?"

Mother said, "You have had a big day.
But you children did not get to eat
Dick's birthday cake.
Here it is."

Dick said, "This is a big day for me!
I had one birthday cake, Mother.
This yellow cake makes two.
Let's all go in and eat this one now."

Soon Father said, "Come, children.
It is time to take you home."

The children ran to thank Grandfather
and Grandmother.
"Thank you for a good day," they said.
"We like to come to your farm.
We want to come back soon."

Then they all got in the car.
"What a day!" said Pete.
"What a day we have had!"

Fun at the Zoo

Father said, "Here is the children's zoo.
The pets and farm animals are in here."

The girls wanted to see the pets.
So did Dick and Pete.
But Billy wanted to see the farm animals.

"Come on, Billy," said Dick.
"We will all look at the farm animals.
Then we will go to see the pets."

Billy looked at all the farm animals.

He saw a mother pig and her little pigs.

He saw a hen and her little chickens.

Then he came to a big cow.

Billy wanted to ride on the cow.

Dick's father laughed.

"You can't ride a cow, Billy," he said.

"Let's go and look at the zoo pets.

Maybe you can ride on a pet."

"See this little animal," said Jane.

"It likes to have me pet it.

It wants to make friends with us."

Sally said, "Hello, little one.

You are so pretty.

I want to pet you, too."

"Look at that!" said Pete.
"Two boys are on that pet.
What a funny ride that is!"

Dick laughed and laughed.
"Come here, Billy," he called.
"Here is a funny pet you can ride."

Sally said, "Oh, Billy!
Let me ride with you."

"Jump on, Sally," said Jane.
"You and Billy take a ride,
but come back soon.
I want to ride that funny pet, too.
So do Pete and Dick."

All the children had a ride.

Then Sally said, "It was fun to ride
a zoo pet.

Now let's ride a big zoo animal."

"Oh, no," laughed Pete.

"We can look at the big animals.

But we can't ride them, and we
can't pet them."

Fun with Friends

Dick said, "I am a big zoo animal.

Who can guess what I am?

I can hop like a rabbit.

But I am not a rabbit.

Look in my animal book.

You will see zoo animals in there.

Find what I am."

The children all looked in the book.

Jane said, "Here are big animals,

but I don't see one that hops."

"I am in there," said Dick.

"Try to find me, Jane."

Soon Jane said, "Oh, look here.

Now I know what Dick is.

We saw this animal at the zoo."

Tom said, "Now guess what I am.

I am a big, big animal.

All the children go to see me

at the zoo.

It is fun to see me eat.

What animal am I?

Can you find me in the book?"

Sally laughed and laughed.

"Oh, Tom," she said.

"It is easy to guess what you are.

I saw you at the zoo.

I can find you in the book.

Here you are."

Pete said, "I am a big animal.
Who can guess what I am?"

Billy said, "Are you a cow?"

"No, no!" said Pete.
"I am not a farm animal.
I am a zoo pet.
You saw me in the children's zoo."

Susan said, "Oh, Pete.
It is not easy to guess
what you are."

"I am in the book," said Pete.
"Let Jane help you look for me.
She saw me at the zoo."

Jane said, "Here you are, Pete.
We had a ride on your back
at the children's zoo."

Soon Pete and Billy's mother called
to the boys.

"Please come home now," she said.

Billy said, "Let me ride home, Pete.
I want to ride on your back."

Away went Pete and Billy.
Then Tom and Susan went home, too.

Dick said, "What good friends we have!
What fun we have with them!"